To Vicky,
Grandma loves spending time with you !! :)

To Vicky,
Grandma loves spending time with you !! :)

Valy Jason

Printed in the United States of America
ISBN 978-1-64133-609-3 (sc)
ISBN 978-1-64133-608-6 (e)

Library of Congress Control Number: 2019908050

Children's Book
19.07.01

AuthorCentrix
25220 Hancock Ave #300,
Murrieta, CA 92562

www.authorcentrix.com

 AuthorCentrix

Making Cookies with Grandma

with Grandma

Joey's Family Collection

Being a Problem Solver

Valy Larson

It was a hot day at Grandma's. Joey and Grandma put on their bathing suits to run through the sprinkler. Grandma took off her watch and set it on the open windowsill.

"Hurray," shouted Joey as he leaped back and forth through the spray.

"Yippee," shouted Grandma as she tiptoed through the sprinkling water.

When Joey and Grandma were totally soaked, they sat on the lawn chairs to dry off. The sun made them feel warm and comfy. After they were dry, they went inside to make some cookies.

But when Grandma went to get her watch, it was gone.

"How very odd," said Grandma, "my watch is gone."

"Don't worry, Grandma. I'll help you look for it," said Joey.

So Joey and Grandma looked for the watch. They looked under the cushions, in the drawers, and under the rug. They looked in the dog basket, between the magazines, and behind the furniture. By the time they finished looking, the living room was a complete mess.

But they could not find the watch.

"Here Grandma," said Joey, "you can use my watch."

"Thank you," said Grandma. "This will help me take the cookies out of the oven right on time!"

Joey and Grandma got ready to make the cookies. Grandma put on her red apron, and Joey put on his white apron with a big pocket in the front. They took turns putting all the ingredients in a big bowl.

Then they mixed the ingredients together with their hands to make the cookie dough. Joey had to put a little more flour in the bowl because the dough was too sticky. Finally the dough was ready to roll out.

9

But when Grandma was rolling out the dough, her necklace got caught in the rolling pin.

"Oh! My necklace is stuck," said Grandma.

"Don't worry, Grandma. I'll help you get it unstuck," said Joey.

"Thank you," said Grandma.

Joey helped Grandma clean the necklace and she put it on the open windowsill.

After that, Grandma had no trouble rolling out the dough. Joey used the cookie cutter to make three dogs, two cats, and one horse. And the rest of the cookies were stars and circles.

Then Grandma put the cookies inside the oven to bake.

"Mmm, they smell good," said Joey.

When the cookies were golden brown, Grandma took them out of the oven. While the cookies were cooling, Joey and Grandma cleaned up the kitchen. Then Grandma went to put on her necklace.

But her necklace was gone.

"I can't believe that," said Grandma. "My necklace is gone."

"Don't worry Grandma. I'll help you look for it," said Joey.

So Joey and Grandma looked in the sink, on the counters, and in the drawers. They looked under the table, in the cat's dish, and in Grandma's pockets. By the time they finished looking in the kitchen, it was a complete mess.

But they could not find the necklace.

Poor Grandma looked sad and worn-out.

So Joey thought about this for a while.

"Grandma," he said, "let's put your earrings on the windowsill and see what happens."

"Okay," said Grandma. "That's a good idea!"

So after Joey put Grandma's earrings on the windowsill, they hid under the table with some milk and cookies. They waited quietly as they munched their cookies and sipped their milk.

Slowly, two black eyes, and a black nose with white whiskers, appeared over the windowsill. Quick as a wink the thief hopped onto the windowsill and grabbed the earrings. In no time the thief was gone.

Grandma and Joey climbed onto the counter to look out of the window.

"It's a raccoon," said Joey.

"Well isn't that a bunch of flimflam!" said Grandma.

"Come on, let's follow it," said Joey.

But by the time Grandma and Joey climbed out the window to follow the raccoon, it was nowhere in sight.

So Joey thought about this for a while.

"Grandma", said Joey, "I have an idea. Let's catch the raccoon in a trap and take it to the woods with the other raccoons. That way it won't steal your things any more."

"That's a clever idea!" said Grandma.

So Joey and Grandma set a trap in the back yard. Joey put some tasty dog food in the trap. Then they went inside the house to have another cookie.

A little while later they heard a bang.

Joey and Grandma rushed outside to look in the trap, but they did not find a raccoon. Instead, they had trapped the neighbor's dog.

"Well that's a bit of nonsense," said Grandma.

So Joey thought about this for a while.

"This time let's try putting cat food in the trap," said Joey.

"Okay," said Grandma. "That's a smart idea!"

Joey took the neighbor's dog home. Then he put some cat food inside the trap and carefully propped open the door. Joey and Grandma went back inside the house to finish their cookie.

A little while later they heard a bang.

Joey and Grandma rushed outside to look in the trap. But, they did not find a raccoon, or the neighbor's dog. Instead, they had trapped Grandma's cat and kitten.

"Well that's some bamboozle," said Grandma.

So Joey thought about this for a while.

"Grandma, I have an idea. Let's put your bracelets inside the trap."

"Okay," said Grandma. "That's a crafty idea!"

Joey let Grandma's cat and kitten go. Then he put Grandma's shiny bracelets inside the trap and carefully propped open the door. Joey and Grandma went back inside the house to have one more cookie.

A little while later they heard a bang.

Joey and Grandma rushed outside to look in the trap.

"We caught the raccoon!" said Joey.

"We did it!" said Grandma.

They sat on the grass and talked about how to take the raccoon to the woods.

Joey and Grandma lifted the trap onto the red wagon. Then they pulled the wagon into the woods along the path.

When they came to a hollow log they opened the cage door and let the raccoon go. The raccoon happily scampered into the hollow log.

Joey and Grandma said good-bye to the raccoon and walked back home.

When Joey was walking up the steps to the house, he noticed something shiny under the deck.

Joey and Grandma crawled on their hands and knees under the deck. And there in an old doghouse was a nest of shiny objects with a half-eaten cookie and some dog food scattered on the ground.

"Look," said Joey, "here are your missing things!"

"And look," said Grandma. "Here are Grandpa's missing glasses!"

"I know just what Grandpa would say," said Joey. "How did they get in there?"

Joey and Grandma smiled, and went back inside the house. Then they set out some cookies and milk for Grandpa and Joey's younger sister, Rosy. The two of them would soon be home from Rosy's summer camp.

Next, Joey helped Grandma clean up the living room and the kitchen. At last, they snuggled together on the couch to read a good book – all about raccoons.

CPSIA information can be obtained
at www.ICGtesting.com
Printed in the USA
LVHW070237070819
626587LV00028B/69/P